Adventures of Tobah

Adventures of Tobah

Wendy L. Jackson

AUCTOREM
HOUSE

Auctorem House
276 5th Ave, Ste 704-2591
New York, NY 10001
www.auctoremhouse.com
Phone: 1 888-332-7718

Published by Auctorem House: 11/26/2024

ISBN: 978-1-965687-08-6(sc)
ISBN: 978-1-965687-09-3(e)

Library of Congress Control Number: 2024919238

Chapter One

Tobah's feet were the only part of him visible as he was head-first in the human boys' toy box. He was looking for that soldier doll's parachute. He totally forgot to put on his own parachute before he left home this morning which wasn't like him at all. Now he was in a hurry to leave the human house and needed the parachute to make a quick get-away. He knew it was here somewhere, he'd just seen it a week ago.

He was starting to run out of time, they'd be home from school soon and he'd already pushed his luck too many times.

"Come on," he said out loud, crawling out of the mess of stuffed toys, GI Joe dolls and blocks, "where haven't I looked?" As his eyes scanned the room, he spotted it! Under the bed! Of course! Any time he didn't see anything for a while it was under the bed. Messy boys!

He ran full speed to grab it up which took a while since he was only two inches high. "I hope it isn't ripped," he said out loud. Tobah was always talking to himself. He hooked the white cotton parachute around his arm and ran with it toward the closet for cover. But halfway to the closet one of the ropes hooked on a toy truck in the middle of the floor and Tobah's feet came out from under him. Up in the air he went and landed with a thud right on his butt! Whoomp!

"Ohhhhhh *I hate* that!" Tobah yelled. Picking himself up, he then jumped up and down in frustration. He grabbed his red-orange hair and pulled straight up. Then he made that high-pitched screaming sound through his lips he makes when he's particularly frustrated. The sight is so hilarious everyone who sees it laughs out loud, even if Tobah appears to be in dire straits! Tobah doesn't laugh though.

Brushing himself off and picking up the parachute, Tobah made it to the closet where he opened up the parachute to make sure there were no tears in it before he used it. He always took cover unless he was on the move. If the children came home from school and he didn't hear them come in, it's better to be in the closet than on the open floor and have to run for cover. They'd see him immediately, whereas if he was in the closet he could hide in there until it was safe to go home.

The G.I. Joe parachute was dirty but not ripped. He didn't have time to fold it properly, he could only throw it over the landing and hope for the best. He had to make it past the front door before they came home or else he'd have to use the stairs and that was *so hard*! And he'd have to wait until they'd all gone to bed so he wouldn't be seen.

He bolted to the landing and tied the waist cord around him tightly. Then he gathered up the parachute fabric, crossed his fingers, said a quick prayer, and hurled it over the landing. Then he jumped through the banisters after it and prayed even harder. "Please open, please open, please open…" Tobah prayed.

It was not opening. "Oh my God," Tobah said, "I'm going to hit the floor. The *marble* floor." His back pack was full of heavy things, pulling him down faster and faster but he didn't have time to take it off.

Suddenly he was thinking of Bellah and the argument they'd had at breakfast that morning. That's what made him forget his parachute. She was such a pain in the neck to Tobah. Very immature. Of course, she was younger than he was but she just got on his nerves all the time. He wondered how anyone could have a girlfriend at all, but to think about Bellah as a girlfriend. . . he shivered. Ugh. No way.

Just then, the parachute *did* open with no time to spare and Tobah dropped to the floor much harder than he would've liked, but it was better than splattering onto the marble. His heart was beating so fast he thought it would explode, but he didn't have time to sit and rest.

He quickly gathered up the parachute and ran, parachute strings flying behind him, toward his exit. That's when he heard the key in the doorknob and voices on the other side. "I'm *not going to make it in time!!*" he thought.

He ran as fast as he possibly could. His legs were moving so fast he almost fell backward. He got to the baseboard just as both of the boys stepped into the foyer of the house. He whipped open the door and ran through.

Timothy was the guard on duty this afternoon. "Oh. Hi," he said to Timothy, pushing the door shut behind him with a bang. He leaned against the door, his legs a little rubbery underneath him from such a bolt of energy and the long run.

Tobah stood there silently panting, his heart about to burst, and he listened. The boys were still talking about some girl on the playground who fell off the monkey bars and one of them saw her underwear. They didn't stop talking and Tobah knew that he hadn't been seen. If he had been, they would've stopped talking for sure, and stared toward the door where Timothy was looking intently through the peep hole.

"Hi Tobah," said Timothy. "Everything…" the guard paused for a length of time, "okay?" Tobah knew he'd be spoken to about this close call now. Timothy blabs to everyone about everything

"Yeah!!" said Tobah. "Couldn't be better! How are you? How's the new baby, Timothy? You're not getting a lot of sleep I bet. Is he talking yet? Sure is a cute baby." Tobah was rambling, which he did when he was nervous.

"Baby's great, Tobah. Yeah, not talking yet as he's still only a month old." replied Timothy, sarcastically.

"Oh, only a month huh? Funny how time flies. Well, I gotta go," and with that Tobah turned and ran.

He knew he couldn't take chances like that anymore. If he weren't more careful he was going to get seen and that would be the end of it for the clan. They'd have to leave the human house fast and leave everything behind. Being found out by the humans is the worst thing to happen to a clan of Plinkets. They have to grab their stash of food and medical supplies and get out of the house fast before the humans find their home. That's how Plinkets live in our houses without us knowing about it, they're very careful not to ever be seen.

Tobah walked through the narrow passageways behind the human house walls, passing other Plinkets on his way to his room where he threw the parachute on the bed. He took off his backpack and took out a big chunk of chocolate chip cookie he gathered today and stuffed it into his mouth, being careful not to drop any crumbs on his bed. Then he put the backpack back on so he could give Cookie the rest of the stuff in it. It was all kitchen stuff today.

When he got to the kitchen Cookie was alone and glad to see him. "Oh good, I hope you remembered the butter Tobah! We're almost out altogether." Cookie was the clan's cook and one of the Elders. He had a particularly soft spot in his heart for Tobah, not just because Tobah was the Gatherer, but because of his circumstances, being orphaned as a small child and Cookie taking him in and raising him.

Tobah said, "I remembered it," and plopped his over-sized back pack on the counter. He took the large container with the lid out of his back pack that held the butter he'd scooped into it and handed it to Cookie. Then he began to pull things out of the backpack and placing them on the counter. First was a container of vanilla pudding, probably tonight's dessert. Then came a container of milk, a rolled up slice of bacon and a folded up slice of pre-wrapped cheese. Tobah was proud of how much stuff he could get into his backpack.

Now Tobah took the time to ask Cookie for the hundredth time, where in the world his wrist watch was that he had asked for.

"*Why* is it *taking* so *long*, Cookie?" Tobah whined. "I really need the watch bad."

Cookie was starting to get annoyed at Tobah's constant whining about the package he was expecting in the mail, but he had word that it would arrive any day now. The mailman told him he heard something really special was coming to the clan and would be here tomorrow or the next day. Cookie didn't tell Tobah this though because he knew he would still whine about it anyway.

"Tobah," Cookie said, "why have you no patience at all? It's not even Plinket-like to not have any patience. You are the most impatient Plinket I've ever met in my life!"

"But Cookie! I almost got seen again today. I can't see the clock by their bed and that's where I was this afternoon."

Cookie questioned him, "Why were you in their bedroom? What could we need from there?" He was suspecting for days now that

Tobah goofed off out in the house more than he gathered. But he wanted to give him the benefit of the doubt. Tobah was, after all, the best Gatherer he's ever known of.

"I, um, well, you see," Tobah stuttered, "Well I had to have a new parachute because I ripped the old one again and Bellah said pretty soon it won't have any integrity and won't hold me up so I needed a new one. It's a doll's parachute for one of their toys, they call them action figures."

Cookie didn't know why on earth Tobah would need a parachute and asked him so. "Tobah, why in the world do you need to be on the 2nd floor of the house anyway? Do you use a parachute to get back to the 1st floor? Isn't that dangerous? What if it didn't open and you were laying there on the floor when they came home? You'd be hurt and seen and couldn't get to us to tell us you'd been seen."

Tobah was starting to get frustrated. He felt that itchy feeling on his head whenever he felt this way but resisted the urge to pull on his hair. He knew where this was going, they were going to make him have a partner. He knew his freedom out in the human house would be short-lived.

"Cookie," Tobah said, "I have to have the parachute to land on the 1st floor from the 2nd floor because it takes too long to take the stairs down. And I have to go to the 2nd floor because that's where they keep the Q-tips and the scotch tape."

Cookie looked at Tobah, his eyes squinting just a tiny bit, and wondered why there would be no scotch tape in the office on the first floor. He was about to ask Tobah that when Tobah said, "They probably have scotch tape in the office on the first floor but the drawer of the desk is too heavy for me to get open. I think they have paper clips in there, too, so I've really tried and tried to get the drawer open. I need some kind of pry bar or something – something that won't leave a mark on the wooden desk for them to notice."

Cookie knew how important Q-tips were for the clan. Everyone cleaned every day and Q-tips made it easy to clean the ceilings of their cubbies. He decided he'd leave it alone and let Tobah decide where in the house he should go. But he wasn't happy about the parachute idea. And doubly not happy that Tobah gathered alone. It wasn't safe.

"Tobah," he said, "Please promise me you will always be very careful parachuting to the lower floor. If you got hurt none of us would know until it was too late. I worry about you Choo Choo."

Tobah loved it when Cookie called him by his special nickname. He got it when he was very young. He had a toy train and played with it *everywhere*. Cookie came upon him in the pantry pushing his train along the floor and chanting, 'choo-choo, choo-choo, choo-choo' and started calling him that. The name stuck and now that Tobah is almost 15 he still loves it when Cookie calls him that. It reminds him of his long lost parents.

"I promise, Cookie. I'm always very careful. I don't want to get hurt, either."

Cookie handed Tobah a cupcake that had just come out of the oven then. Tobah's eyes got wide as he started to unwrap the paper lining, "Thank you, Cookie!"

Cookie said, "You skedaddle on out of here now, I'm about to get busy making dinner. And you should see your package in the next day or two. A little birdie told me."

Tobah said thank you but his mouth was full of warm cupcake and little crumbs came out of his mouth when he spoke. Cookie looked at him disapprovingly and Tobah just waved a little apology and got up to leave the kitchen.

Back in his room, Tobah unfurled the whole new parachute and inspected it again for any rips or tears. The old one was mended so many times there were lines of stitching crisscrossed all over it. Bellah was the one who mended it as she was the new apprentice and needed the practice of making neat stitches. She was very good at it already and Tobah admired her ability. She was a little mean to him though. He didn't like that.

As Tobah went hand over hand over the whole parachute he found that it was in perfect condition. Good. He carefully packed it into his old parachute pack – he only had one of those – so it was ready to use. Then he took his old parachute, packed it carefully into the box Cookie had given him, labeled the outside "Tobah's old parachute" and picked up the box to make his way down to the storage area. He pulled the curtain of his room open and *surprise*! Bellah was standing there! Staring right in his face.

"*Oh no*," he thought, "*what does she want now*?" He cocked his head to the side and just said, "What?"

"We all know, Tobah! We all know how you almost got caught again today." Bellah practically spit the words out at him. "Timothy overheard you talking to Cookie and now we all know. If you don't start being careful you're going to get caught and then what will happen, Tobah?! We'll have to move away and leave everything behind! And it'll all be *your fault*!"

Tobah looked at her, cocked his head to the other direction and just said, "Bellah, you are so dramatic you should be in movies." He took a step toward her and she stepped out of his way.

"Oh yeah?" Bellah said, as Tobah started down the hall, "well. . .

Maybe I *will*!" not having anything better to say. She thought Tobah would put up some kind of defensive fight and found she was quite disappointed that he didn't. She liked fighting with Tobah. After all, no one will fight with you if they don't like you and care about your opinions. And Bellah liked Tobah more than she cared to admit. And more than Tobah would ever believe.

Tobah walked past her, box under one arm, threw up the other hand in the air and said, "Go ahead! Go be in a stupid human movie! Then who will get caught, huh?"

Bellah was sad all of a sudden, seeing him walk away, but she didn't know why. She felt something she was starting to become familiar with. It was a kind of loneliness when he wasn't around.

Bellah's mother would be most disheartened to learn of this, as she'd told Bellah before she would not allow Bellah to be partnered with a Gatherer. Too dangerous. Especially Tobah as unruly as she heard he is. No way Bellah would be partnered with Tobah. No, she was thinking she would partner her daughter with Enid. He worked the gardens and was very reliable and hard-working. Not quite as dangerous working in the gardens as it was gathering. Dangerous, still, just not *as* dangerous.

Tobah and his clan are always in danger of being seen by humans. It's a built-in worry that the Plinkets have long since learned to live with ever since they came out of the forests. It's why when a baby Plinket is born it doesn't cry and scream like human babies do. Plinkets are very, very quiet. If you were smack in the middle of a den of Plinkets, you might not even know it. Of course if you were the same size as they are it would seem much, much different. You would hear how loud they really are among themselves, but still too quiet for humans to hear.

And where they live helps them. They live in the walls and

floorboards of human houses. It won't do any good to pull up all your floor boards to see, though. Their special kind of magic makes it seem to humans as if you're just seeing in a kind of dream state. You might see them or their dwelling but to you it wouldn't look real. You would just shake your head and feel that you'd just woken up from a day dream. And then right away you would forget all about it like it never happened.

This magic is built in to the Plinket's world and in their behavior. They rely on it all the time, but they don't rely on it *alone*. Their quietness is what keeps them from being discovered. That, and not being seen in broad daylight while gathering a parachute from under a bed. It's the Gatherers, the Gardeners, and the Hunters who are most likely to be seen.

After he'd returned to his room from putting the old parachute into storage, Tobah started washing up for dinner. Tonight Cookie was serving his special African Hot Dish and Tobah *loved* Cookie's African Hot Dish. It was so good that Tobah would give up gathering if he could eat it all day and night. Of course then he would be too big to gather anyway, but it was a little daydream Tobah had. There he was, lying all stretched out on his belly in a *giant* bowl of African Hot Dish shoveling hands full of the stuff into his mouth. Mmmmmmmmm, he started rubbing his hands even faster with the soap and water.

Pretty soon there were bubbles all around his sink and water spraying everywhere. Plinkets hated dirtiness or messiness. Now Tobah would be late for dinner cleaning up his mess.

"Ohhhhhhh I hate that!" Tobah said out loud. He looked around at the mess and started jumping up and down, pulling on his hair straight up over his head like he does when he's frustrated. Tobah has fiery orangey red hair – he's the only one in the clan with hair that color. Everyone else's hair is brown or black or blonde but

Tobah is different. Nobody knows where Tobah's hair color came from. It's rumored that the Leader of the Plinkets has that same hair color but no one really knows for sure. And wouldn't that be funny if unruly, impatient, and weird little Tobah had physical characteristics of the Great Leader!

Dropping to his knees with a rag, Tobah started wiping up the soapy water he splashed all around. "Stupid daydream anyway," he was saying to himself, "like Cookie could make up a whole human sized bowl of African Hot Dish just for me and still have enough to feed everyone else too."

Rinsing and wringing out his rag as he cleaned up the soap bubbles and water, he realized that his room was actually a lot dirtier than he thought it was. He quickly wiped his rag over all the surfaces of his room, except his bed cover and his sofa and his chair, which were upholstered with very nice brocade fabric, and then was very happy at the sight. Realizing he was late for dinner, he ran out of his room and down the hall to the dining room.

Chapter Two

The next day, while gathering in the human kitchen, Tobah looked up at the big digital clock on the microwave. 8 am. Good! He had all day to gather if he wanted to. And he was going to get Cookie a surprise today – one of George's shirts! It would be hard, sure, but Tobah wanted to show his appreciation to Cookie for everything he did for him. Just one of George's shirts would make 4 new table cloths for the dining room tables and that would make Cookie so happy!

Cookie always made sure the tables were set for dinner; all the silver was always kept polished by the kitchen workers, the dishes and glassware were shiny and clean, cloth napkins were always used – never paper napkins or paper towels except for when it's an Off Day or a picnic, but never, never was the table without a table cloth. Cookie had half a dozen of them, all different patterns and colors and the napkins matched their own table cloths. But Cookie would love it if all three tables matched each other. That would be an awesome thing to him.

It took the launderettes a long time to iron one of the large tablecloths and 4 ironing boards all set up in a square to accommodate the size of just one of them. There were 50 Plinkets in Tobah's clan and they had three long dining room tables to accommodate all of them. There were about 16 Plinkets per table, depending on where the younger ones wanted to sit, either with their friends or with their family.

Oh, Cookie would be so happy to have new table cloths! The truth of the matter is, Tobah wasn't doing it just because of the extra portions Cookie always gave him, or the treats here and there, or the good advice Tobah almost always took, it was mostly because of the package he was expecting to get any day now. Cookie had a big hand in making that wish come true and Tobah was very grateful for Cookie's help.

Tobah wouldn't have received such a gift just by asking for it on his own. They would've scoffed at him! "Hmph," they would have said, "You don't need it! Just pay more attention to what you're doing!" But Cookie knew that Tobah really needed this gift, that Tobah got carried away and lost track of time while he was out gathering. He was safe, Cookie was sure of that or he would've been caught years earlier. But Tobah was a special Gatherer. He brought home things other Gatherers don't usually think of. And for that Cookie thought Tobah should be rewarded.

You see, the Gatherer is the only Plinket allowed to go out into the human house. Sometimes the Gatherer has an apprentice, but Tobah went alone. Their humans had a cat in the house which made gathering even more dangerous. Cats used to love to eat Plinkets. In fact, that's what drove the Plinkets out of their beloved forests and into the homes of humans. The humans would let their cat outdoors, the cat would mate with a stray cat, lots of baby kitties were born and roamed around the land free to go wherever they wanted to, like in the woods where all the Plinkets were!

It got to be too dangerous for them to live outside unprotected so they started, one clan after another, moving into human houses. Even if the humans had a cat in the house, it only endangered the Gatherer, not the whole clan. And the Gatherer had a special cat repellant spray on his person at all times when he was out in the house. It was in a container just like joggers carry when they jog on a trail – it's kind of like a mace spray but specially made by Plinkets for cats and mice and whenever the family dog gets too curious. Cats hate it and it knocks them out asleep for hours at a time. They developed the cat repellant from the time when there were saber tooth tigers roaming north America. That's how strong it is – it will knock out a saber tooth tiger.

If you ever come home from school and find that your cat is really sleepy or woozy – you can bet he got sprayed by a Plinket! Most cats have learned instinctually to avoid Plinkets now but there are still some stupid ones here and there that need to be 'reminded' with the spray. After a few good sprays, the cats leave the Gatherers alone. For the most part. There is still inherent danger every day you have a cat in the midst.

Tobah was in the human kitchen now, and pried the refrigerator open with his fridge-opening tool. He climbed up to the bottom shelf. Then he took his rope and hook and hurled it up to the top shelf. Got it! Then he climbed the rope until he could reach the egg carton. He had a heck of a time getting the egg out of the refrigerator but Cookie was nearly out of freeze dried eggs and so Tobah had no choice. He always got Cookie whatever he needed, danger or not. And trying to get out of a fridge with an egg in your back pack was dangerous, believe it. He had to swing way out away from the shelf on his rope and not crack the egg on any shelves on his way down.

He'd made some messes in the beginning that's for sure. But he was pretty good at it now. He got tired of cleaning up all the egg messes so the humans wouldn't see that something was amiss. They never noticed when eggs were missing, but they would sure notice if one were broken all over a shelf inside their fridge or dripping onto the floor!

So Tobah made it down safely, whipped his rope up and off the shelf and coiled it back up on his hip. Then he made his way for home to drop off the egg. He always made two or three trips out into the house on his gathering days, but when he had to get an egg, there was always an extra trip just for that. It was *heavy*! Instead of carrying it on his back in his backpack, he usually rolled it home.

He got the egg through the door and down the hallways to the kitchen where the kitchen workers would crack it open into the largest of the tubs and whisk it all up. He watched them once, fascinated they knew what to do with it. Cookie said it's from generations of passing down information so all food is handled safely and no one gets sick. Tobah sometimes wished he was a kitchen worker because he loved to eat – but Cookie said kitchen workers don't just get to eat all day. The food the Gatherer brings in is for the whole clan, not a select few.

The kitchen workers would then pour the whisked egg into very large cookie sheets that had an edge all the way around them and were so big they had to be carried by two Plinkets at once. Then they walked them to the walk-in freezer and placed them on shelves until they freeze-dried. Cookie said that means they stay out in the open, without any plastic wrap or lid on them so the liquid will evaporate off as it cools. Then – voila! Eggs whenever you want them. After the egg is all dried out the workers scrape it off the trays and into special barrels Cookie has for the eggs. Then the barrels are stacked inside the pantry for future use.

Cookie goes through a lot of eggs. He believes the clan should be treated to dessert every night after dinner. Everyone works really hard to keep the clan in food and clothing and shoes and every other item they need, and Cookie is a very loving Cookie indeed. Some other clans' Cookies don't make dessert except for special occasions. One might get a small cake on one's birthday, for instance. But Tobah's clans' Cookie is awesome, so Tobah doesn't mind bringing eggs back home even though they're heavy and cumbersome.

After Tobah's break in the kitchen watching the workers prepare the egg for drying, he ate a little bite that Cookie always made him for his first break. It was usually some protein and sugar, such as, a piece of bacon and a cookie, or an egg sandwich and a cup of hot chocolate. The Gatherer of the clan always got more food than everyone else because he used up so many calories doing the gathering.

After his snack Tobah left the kitchen and headed back to the inside of the humans' house. He was going to have to get going up the stairs if he was going to do the enormous task of finding a shirt for Cookie's tablecloths. He got to the door in the side of the wall and hung out for a minute like he usually did, listening to make sure no one was around. He ran to the stairs and flung his hook up onto the carpeted stair and then hoisted himself up, one step at a time until he was at the top of the stairs. He sat and rested for ten minutes to catch his breath. He loved to lay on the landing in the sun from the window and day dream about his weird dreams he has at night. Last night he dreamt about dinosaurs again and he wished he knew what it meant. He'd never seen a real dinosaur and only saw them in books, so he didn't understand why he dreamt about them so often. Weird.

Finally in the master bedroom, Tobah was on the top shelf in the clothes closet picking out a shirt to make Cookie's new table cloths. He chose a white cotton fabric that had blue stripes through it. He'd been keeping tabs on it now for 6 months. George never wore it the whole time it was hanging in there so that's how he picked which one. Might not miss something you never wear. It was awesome! And around the collar and cuffs was a blue denim colored fabric that would work perfect for the matching napkins. Cookie would be so excited!! Good thing George was a big human or there wouldn't be enough fabric to do this. Tobah would tell Bellah to make the table cloths out of the back of the shirt so there would be no seams in them, just neat hemming. The front two pieces would be used for the other two tablecloths.

He would like to get out to the garage and get some of those o-rings for napkin rings but going out there was way too dangerous and he only did that when it was absolutely necessary. The garage countertops out there were higher than they are in the kitchen, and it's a concrete floor he would land on instead of the soft throw rugs around the kitchen, if he fell. Most things they needed could be found in the house.

Tobah got the shirt off the hanger by falling onto it from above, and unbuttoning it and, with the collar in one hand, climbing over the hanger so one side of the shirt slid off. Then he climbed down the shirt tail closer to the floor and the weight of him pulled the rest of the shirt off the hanger. Tobah plopped down onto the carpeted closet floor and started gathering up the shirt. He stuffed the shirt into his backpack the best he could and trotted off out of the bedroom and down the hallway to the landing.

He barely stopped before he leapt off the landing, pulling the cord on his parachute on the way down. With the parachute in front like a fanny pack on the wrong way, Tobah could land on whatever was in his back pack, thus ensuring a fairly soft landing, depending on what he was toting home. He didn't like not being able to see his way down to the floor but it was okay.

Tobah ran through the door to home – there was Timothy again – and down the hall to the Seamster's Shop. He ran fast past the kitchen so Cookie wouldn't see the shirt partially hanging out of his backpack. He was met by Bellah and he explained what he wanted her to do with it. She said she'd be happy to make the tablecloths herself and she should be done with them within 3 months.

"No!" Tobah said to Bellah, "I want them to be sewed on the machines so it'll be done faster. I want him to have it this week. If you hem them by hand it'll take such a long time!"

"No way, Tobah! I have to stitch it by hand in my room at night because we have a million things going on right now. We're sewing the costumes for the play and the deadline is in 3 days! We also have a lot of mending to do to the Gardeners' uniforms and we're still mending some of the uniforms for the Hunters and making new uniforms for the new Hunter. We're very busy!"

Tobah pushed his way past her and found Debbie, the head Seamstress, in the midst of all the tables and sewing machines and sewers. "Debbie, will you please help me?" Debbie loved Tobah. And this made Bellah so mad her face turned red.

Bellah was right on Tobah's heels, "I'm sorry, Miss Debbie, I tried to tell him how busy we are but he just doesn't care!"

"There now, Bellah, don't you worry about how busy we are, I'll take care of this. Go off and finish the pants you're sewing and let me take care of new business please."

Bellah walked off in a huff and Tobah turned to Debbie – "Oh thank you Debbie! I knew you'd help me. Bellah is so bossy but you're nice."

Debbie said, "Bellah may be bossy, Tobah, but I'm the boss so when you need something you come to me, not to Bellah. Do you understand?"

"Yes, Miss Debbie. I will from now on."

So Tobah explained how he wanted to make new table cloths and napkins for Cookie using the shirt he'd gathered from George but Debbie confirmed what Bellah had said. They were very busy right now this time of year but they would get on it as fast as they could. They only had so many sewing machines and every one of them was being used as it is. Debbie was thinking of even starting a second shift, she said, and looking for volunteers for the cutting and cleaning up.

Tobah was going to have to be patient. Gulp. Something he was NOT good at. But he bit his tongue and thanked Miss Debbie and turned to leave, his head hung low. Debbie stopped him, "Tobah," she said. Tobah turned to look at her. "Cookie will fall to pieces over these new tablecloths and napkins. You did an excellent job picking out the perfect cotton fabric. He'll love them."

Tobah grinned his famous crooked grin then, the one that melted everyone's heart, and left the shop.

Over in his room, he took off his shoes and socks, washed his feet, pulled his curtain shut and laid on his bed. He was only going to shut his eyes for a moment but he was so tired he fell into a deep sleep.

It was about an hour and a half later when he was awakened by the light tapping on his doorway frame. He was startled to see Father Luther standing there.

"Tobah," said Father Luther, with a smile, "you're missing dinner."

"Oh No!" Tobah exclaimed and jumped up so high he hit his head on the top of his room. "Ouch!" he yelled. Then he screamed through his closed lips from the pain and Father Luther burst out laughing. Tobah looked at him quickly, an embarrassed look on his face, and Father Luther said, "Just wash up quickly and come down – we're waiting for you."

When Tobah arrived at the table, everyone turned to look at him. *Everyone.* He felt immediately uncomfortable in the silent room, with all those eyes on him, but then noticed everyone started smiling. He awkwardly made his way to his seat and sat down. His hair was still damp from washing up and stuck out in some places, making him a comical sight indeed. Bellah's little sister started to laugh, "Oh Tobah, you're so silly!!" she said.

Then Cookie tapped on his water glass and everyone sat up straight and waited for him to speak. "We have a special reason to celebrate this evening and I'm going to tell you about it. Our humble Gatherer, Tobah, has received a gift in the mail today and I wanted to share it with the entire clan."

Upon hearing this news Tobah started bouncing up and down on his seat, his hair toppling even more messy and several clan members were laughing now.

"This is a serious matter, ladies and gentlemen," said Cookie. Everyone settled down and he continued, "As you know, our Tobah gathers for us so well but sometimes he pays so much attention to gathering the things our clan has asked for that he loses track of what time it is and our humans don't have but just a couple of clocks in the whole house. As you also know, if Tobah is trapped in the house past a certain time, it becomes too dangerous for him to return home. There are humans in the house after 3 pm and Tobah has to be up and out of there before then in order to not be seen."

Cookie went on, "Because of his attention to our needs and the ways he goes above and beyond his call of duty, I asked the Council for a gift for Tobah to help him while he's out in the house gathering. This is a special gift that is expensive to make and therefore most Plinkets will never see one, but because Tobah is special to us, I asked them to make it happen."

He walked down to where Tobah was seated and handed a box to him then, and said, "Tobah, thank you for being such a wonderful and efficient Gatherer for us. Please accept this gift from the entire clan for your efforts and we hope this will make you even safer when you're out gathering for us." Everyone started to clap and say things like, "Bravo, Tobah," or "Good job," or "You're the best."

Tobah took the box, grinning from ear to ear, and started to remove the brown paper wrapping. Underneath the brown wrapping was a fancy wrapping paper! Bright yellow and pink and turquoise paisley printed paper popped out at him – it was beautiful! It was *so* beautiful Tobah almost forgot what was inside the box.

He removed the paper carefully, as he planned to keep it forever, pressed in his scrap book. Then he cut the tape of the box and opened it up so slowly, and peeked inside. Another box!! He took that box out of the bigger one and opened it up quickly and there before his eyes was the most beautiful gift he ever saw. It was a silver watch with a black leather band. The face of the watch was made of Mother of Pearl and had tiny silver numbers all the way around it.

He stared at it in disbelief, "It's real," he said. He jumped up from the table and hugged Cookie and said, "Put it on me, Cookie! Put it on me!"

Everyone laughed and smiled and congratulated Tobah on his special gift while Cookie attached the watch to Tobah's wrist with the delicate little buckle.

Tobah stared at it, not moving. He couldn't look away, it was so beautiful. Cookie cleared his throat then, and Tobah remembered his manners. He looked up and said, "Thank you everyone, for making this such a special night for me. I'll never forget it." Then all the clan started clapping and Tobah hugged Cookie hard, then made his way back to his seat.

Dinner was served then. Roast Cricket cutlets with gravy and mashed potatoes – a specialty, and there was fresh asparagus and raspberries and whipped cream for dessert. It was an excellent meal in every way. Tobah felt there would never be a better night ever.

When he was in his room after dinner, he flattened out the pretty paisley paper and put it in his scrapbook. Then he wrote on it all about the night and the watch and how Cookie had made it such a special night with his words and what a fabulous meal it had been.

That night as Tobah laid in his bed, rubbing the knot on his head from hitting it on his ceiling earlier, he fell asleep staring at the watch on his wrist and not believing what a lucky Plinket he was.

Chapter Three

Today was Saturday and an Off Day and that meant Tobah didn't have to go gathering and could do whatever he wanted to. Usually on his Off Day he would hook up with his friend Enid and explore the great outdoors. He loved doing this and would often bring his bow and arrow to bring home something for dinner, as well.

Enid was a Gardener which made him the perfect partner for exploring. Whenever they got hungry Enid knew what they could eat and what they couldn't. One thing Tobah loved to eat which he always knew were safe were the blue bell flowers that grew in the woods behind the human's house. Enid thought they were too sweet which suited Tobah just fine – more for him!

As Tobah washed up and got dressed, he decided he would hunt today and bring home some meat. He left his room and headed for the kitchen to see what kind of meat Cookie wanted.

Cookie was busy with breakfast, of course and so Tobah had to make it fast. He didn't like interrupting Cookie but Cookie was *always* busy supervising the cooking of something so not interrupting him was impossible most times, except when he was in the living room or the library at the end of the day and he was usually nodding off into a book.

Cookie was scolding one of the kitchen workers when Tobah walked in, advising him "for the hundredth time" to not stir the muffin batter. "With your spoon, pick up the ingredients from the sides of the bowl and transfer them to the center, like this," as Cookie showed him again how to do it. "That way your muffins won't have tunnels in them."

"Oh I forgot!" said the younger Plinket, "I'm sorry Cookie, I feel like I'm just not cut out for this kind of work." Cookie smiled down at him, "We'll see, son, we'll see."

Cookie smiled to see Tobah standing there with his bow and quiver on his back and his hunting boots and vest on. "That's quite a nice piece of jewelry you have there, Tobah," he said. Tobah looked down at his watch and grinned. "Yeah, I love it," was all he could think of to say. "Cookie, me and Enid are going out today, what kind of meat should I bring home?"

Cookie thought about it for a minute and said, "Squirrel meat. I'll make a nice stew for dinner this week, thank you Tobah! You don't want to spend your Off Day exploring and eating Blue Bell flowers?"

"I thought about it but with Autumn coming I figured we could use the meat or store it in the freezer for Winter time. Besides I like to hunt and I need to work on my bow and arrow skills. I'm probably rusty from not hunting since Springtime. If I can get two of them, Enid can pull one home and then you can make Squirrel Jerky, Cookie!"

Tobah LOVED Squirrel Jerky and there was never enough to go around. Everyone loved Squirrel Jerky. He was determined to bag two squirrels today just for that reason. "I'll get a couple of big ones, Cookie!"

Cookie laughed as Tobah trotted out of the kitchen, "You do that, Tobah, and we'll make some Squirrel Jerky for sure."

Tobah walked toward Enid's family's cubby to find him, passing several other young Plinkets on his way. They walked around with their puzzles or colored pencils and coloring books to enjoy their Off Day activities in the dining room or living room. Tobah was kind of at an in-between age where he missed doing his puzzles and crocheting his blankets, and would sometimes still pull out his yarn and hook and work for a couple of hours on the bedspread he still hasn't finished. He planned on finishing it this Winter when there was little else to do during Off Days. It was a beautiful midnight blue-colored yarn and Tobah was crocheting it in a particularly tight pattern so it would be thick and heavy when it was done. That would help keep him warm during the Winter when it was chilly.

Enid wasn't quite old enough yet to have his own cubby so he still lived with his parents. A Plinket's clan was his family, too, but his mom and dad and brothers or sisters were called his 'natural family' and everyone else was his or her 'clan family.' Plinkets only had one brother or one sister, there were never any more baby Plinkets than two in a family, and usually only one. Enid was an only child like Tobah but Enid still had his parents. Tobah's parents died when he was little in a horrible accident while gathering so Tobah was an orphan. That's why he felt so close to Cookie because Cookie took him in under his wing and helped raise him after his parents were gone. Cookie thought Tobah would train to be a Cookie too, but everyone knew since Tobah's birth that he was a Gatherer. Gatherers are born bigger and stronger than other Plinket babies. Hunters are stronger too. Strong enough at only 2 inches high to drag a full grown squirrel out of the woods and home.

Tobah knocked on the door frame and Enid yelled, "Come on in, Tobah, I'm almost ready." He walked in to find Enid lacing up his boots, a bow and quiver on his back too! "Enid! When did you learn to hunt?" Tobah asked. Enid replied, "I haven't yet, you're going to teach me!"

With that, they both left Enid's family cubby and headed for the kitchen where breakfast would be ready soon. Enid's mom worked in the kitchen with Cookie so Enid always knew what the meal would be and he told Tobah on the way. "Pumpkin bread and scrambled eggs today, Tobah," and Enid was grinning when Tobah looked back at him. Enid could eat all the pumpkin bread in the whole world and it still wouldn't be enough to satisfy him. "Lucky you," Tobah said. He wasn't particularly crazy about pumpkin bread and likes zucchini bread better but he was hungry so it didn't matter that much.

On Off Days the clan would line up in the hall and walk through the kitchen like it was a buffet. Scrambled eggs and chunks of sausage were served in flour wraps so the Plinkets could get their breakfast and eat it on their way out of the kitchen. Plastic cups of orange or grapefruit juice would be available and large bins at the ends of the tables to leave them in when they were done. Plinkets only ate meals in the dining room or the kitchen, nowhere else. That's because if crumbs or spills were left around the place then they would get bugs or rodents. That was very bad for Plinkets who were only two inches tall. Roaches were particularly a problem for Plinkets because they bite and if a clans' messy food habits drew mice or rats into the house, well, you can only imagine what a disaster that would be. A mouse was as tall as most Plinkets so imagine fighting one! When they bite they can take an arm or leg off! Cat repellant works on mice too, for some reason but you have to get dangerously close to it before you can spray it so it's always scary thinking about mice in the house. Tobah wondered who the poor guy was who found that out.

Tobah literally devoured his breakfast, gulped down his juice and was ready to go when he looked back and saw Enid sitting at a table with a plate full of pumpkin bread and a dish of butter. *"Oh no,"* Tobah said to himself, *"we'll never get out of here today."*

He walked up to Enid and said, "Enid! Can't you take it with you? We're just going outside anyway!" Enid looked up, his mouth crammed full of bread and mumbled, "Uh gueth tho," and got up from the table. He then took the other two pieces of bread from the plate and placed them gently into his fanny pack for later on. Which was a very good thing for the both of them, though neither one of them could know the kind of danger they'd be in before night fall. Enid's pumpkin bread would end up sustaining them until morning.

They were finally ready to go outside and as soon as they got out the door Tobah breathed in the air and the sunshine like an inmate just released from prison. He loved being a Gatherer, but he sure loved being outdoors. Sometimes he would lay on the carpet on the upstairs landing in the house on sunny days and soak up the sun like a sponge.

The two Plinkets were halfway into the woods behind the human house when Tobah spotted the first grouping of Blue Bell flowers. Enid looked at Tobah, Tobah looked at Enid, then they both started running to see who would get to them first. Tobah was bigger than Enid and always won but there would come a day when Enid would get to them first. Most Plinkets have a growth spurt at the age Enid is now, though he would never be as tall as Tobah, since Tobah was a Gatherer.

Tobah gently pulled the stem down so he could reach a flower, removed it from the stem, thanked the plant, folded the flower into a little package and popped it into his mouth. Enid laughed every single time at how Tobah's eyes would roll back into his head with delight. "Yuk, Tobah!" he would say, "Why don't you just eat a spoonful of sugar?" and Tobah would always say, "It's not the same thing. The flowers aren't just sweet, they have a flavor. I can't believe you don't like them too. You're the only Plinket I know who doesn't like the taste of Blue Bell flowers."

Tobah then picked another flower, folded it up into a little packet and put it in his fanny pack. Then he picked another and another and performed the same ritual. Deeper into the woods there wasn't enough light for the flowers to grow but he always wanted a snack while they were in there.

As they walked off into the woods Enid asked, "Wanna go to the cave today?"

"No, I'm going to teach you how to practice arrow shooting instead. Here, you stay here and I'll be right back." Tobah walked a little ways into the woods and found a nice round leaf that he leaned against a tree and then walked back to Enid. "Now, pull a bow and hit the center of that leaf with it." Tobah said.

"Ooh what a great idea," said Enid. And so he did what Tobah said, only he didn't hit the leaf in the middle. In fact, he didn't hit the leaf at all, it went whizzing right by it about a foot off the mark. Tobah slapped his hand to his forehead and thought to himself, *"Oh no, the Plinket couldn't hit the broad side of a barn!"* But Enid had already drawn another bow and taken aim. He did hit the leaf that time and almost dead center. He performed the same feat 5 more times, using up all his bows, at which point the two of them walked in to retrieve them.

"You're a natural, Kid!" Tobah said and helped him pick up his bows. "Do you really think so, Tobah? Really? Cuz I'd rather be a Hunter than a Gardener but my dad said I'm too small. Do you think if he saw me shoot arrows he'd change his mind?"

Tobah thought for a minute and said, "Hmmm you'll have to have a talk with him and show him what you can do but being a Hunter is really dangerous for a Plinket. Sometimes it takes more than one arrow to kill an animal and they can attack you before you can get your second arrow shot at them. You will have to practice for a couple of years until you're good enough at three yards before he'd probably let you be a Hunter. But you're really good at it now!"

They walked further into the woods and Tobah would point to something and say, "Shoot that patch of moss," or "Plant one in the middle of that dandelion flower," or "Aim for the knot in that tree," and darned if Enid wouldn't hit the target every time. He really was impressive. "Are you sure you haven't shot a bow and arrow before today?" and Enid assured him he hadn't, but Tobah never heard of a Plinket taking to something so naturally that was so hard to do. Enid really had some upper body strength that Tobah had no idea was there.

And so they walked and shot arrows, the both of them, until they came to the sunny clearing where they liked to stop and rest. After they plopped down on their butts, bouncing up and down on the moss, Enid pulled out a piece of pumpkin bread and Tobah pulled out a folded up Blue Bell flower and they enjoyed their snacks in the sunny spot, laying on the moss and staring at the cloud shapes. "There's a rabbit," Enid said. "Oh, yeah, I see it," said Tobah. "Long ass ears, though."

Enid laughed out loud at that. He always thought it was funny when Tobah used a bad word. Ass. Nobody else Enid knew used that word except Tobah. Maybe when you grow up with no parents you feel comfortable saying 'ass,' he didn't know. But if he said that word in front of his parents, he would be put in a time out for sure. He couldn't wait to be the same age as Tobah so he could say 'ass' too.

Chapter Four

Enid's mom, Lucy, was busy in the pantry doing inventory. She liked to do that on Off Days because she would never be disturbed by people on those days. She could do the inventory, counting the jars of beans or the jars of jam and not be interrupted in the middle and have to start over. It was just easier. And besides, the pantry was her favorite place to be and Off Days were all about doing what you love to do, not what you *had* to do.

The pantry was a giant room with rows and rows of shelves built into the walls. The shelves held all the clans' canned and dried food and inventory was very important. If they were running low on something and didn't realize it, they might not re-stock in time for Winter and the clan would starve then. So Lucy had a system she used to do the inventory. She had all the items already listed down a sheet of paper and she would just put the number of the items on the shelves in a little box next to the item listed. It was so much easier than writing it out every time and this helped her keep the pantry organized as well, which is what Cookie entrusted her to do. Lucy was in charge of the pantry and this was a humongous responsibility. She'd worked with Cookie in the kitchen since she was a teenager. Lucy would probably be the next Cookie when Cookie retired.

The pantry was the most important part of the clans' habitat. It was the biggest cubby of them all and held not only canned items, but dried meats and eggs, barrels of potatoes and long strings of onions tied together hung from the ceiling. There were cans of peas, carrots, beets, pears, asparagus, and all other vegetables they grew in the gardens. There were dried peas in burlap bags, every known kind of pea and bean there was.

There was also a large refrigerator in the pantry that held all the citrus fruit so it wouldn't spoil so soon. It was not all that cold, but just cold enough to keep the lemons and limes and grapefruits from spoiling. They could be kept for weeks and weeks in there. Also there was pineapples and kiwi fruit and cantaloupe melons and pears and peaches and plums and apricots. There were also all kinds of fruit in jars that were made into jelly and jam for toast in the mornings.

Sometimes when things were busy and Lucy needed to do an inventory she would take an apprentice with her to count the jars. Every shop in the clans' world always had at least one or two apprentices learning the job so the older Plinket could retire someday. But the kitchen was different. The kitchen had many apprentices because there was always work to do 24 hours a day in the kitchen. Someone had to be up at four in the morning to start making the bread, then there were people to make breakfast, apprentices to clean up after each meal, cooks who mastered the art of the main course or desserts or pastries and bread, they supervised the apprentices who were learning those trades. And of course there was the midnight meal for the Guard.

A clan always had a Guard on duty at the doorway between the Plinkets home to the human home to alert the clan to danger in case of an emergency. If a Guard's door was breached by an animal or a human, he would alert the clan with his whistle that blew a frequency only the animals or Plinkets could hear, and the clan would gather up what they were supposed to and head for the shelter. The hunters would make their way to the area where the animal was and kill it before it could harm anyone.

For Tobah's clan, the shelter was underneath the floor boards with a narrow passage from underneath, with stairs going up and into the pantry. The clan would then settle down in the shelter, being very quiet, and hoping their home would not be found by humans or animals. With a passage up into the locked pantry they could stay there indefinitely, not having to worry about running out of food for several weeks. If it were a mouse or some other animal that breached the barricade, the Hunters would all stay behind and kill it before it wrecked their cubbies. If it was a human who found them out, they would all meditate together and concentrate on the special magic that kept humans from really seeing what they were looking at. The human would scratch his head, thinking he had seen something and then think, "no, that couldn't be."

As Lucy counted jars, she noticed a grouping of beets whose lids were starting to bow out. "*Oh no,*" she thought, "*bad beets.*" She picked one up and inspected it. "Yep," she said out loud, "tiny bubbles inside." That meant the food inside had fermented and was no good anymore. She set them on the floor away from the other jars because if they exploded they would make a mess on all the other jars near them. They would have to be dumped out and thrown away. How sad, Lucy thought, because of the hard work that went into harvesting and canning the beets, and now they were wasted. Cookie would be very upset. Seven jars of beets had gone bad, the whole batch.

As the Gardeners came in in the afternoons from work they would each have one or two burlap bags of fruit or vegetables they'd harvested that day. Cookie would already have the jars sterilized and waiting to be filled. The giant cooking pots would be filled with water and a nice fire made underneath them for boiling the water. Then the fruit and vegetables would be washed, trimmed, and cut up into the desired size pieces for canning. Off into the boiling water they would go, to parboil and kill any bacteria that remained on the food after washing it.

Then the apprentices would fill the jars, pouring the boiling water over the fruit or vegetables to the top of the jar, a flat lid was then placed on top and the jar would be set into a shallow pan of boiling water for however many minutes was required until it could be removed and set aside. Over time, the food and liquid in the jar would cool which would create a vacuum that would hold the lid tightly over the jar. Then a threaded band would go over that, gently.

If these bands were screwed on too tightly they would break the seal under the lid and the food inside the jar would slowly spoil over time. That's what happened to the beets Lucy found in the pantry. And that's how a whole clan was wiped out one year from bad canning. The kitchen workers and apprentices always thought Cookie was too hard on the apprentices, but there was a reason for this. If they did not can food the exact proper way, the whole clan was in jeopardy of food poisoning.

The whole McCardle clan was wiped out this way, back in the early thirties. Cookie was a very old Plinket and most of the kitchen workers never heard the story. Cookie doesn't share it except with the senior kitchen staff so they know the importance of his rules. The other workers don't need to know until they're older and have more responsibility, for it is the stuff of nightmares.

Lucy was almost done with her inventory when her husband came into the pantry, which he'd never done before. She was so concentrated on her work and so startled by his presence that she dropped her clipboard. "What is it, Darling?" she asked. He said, "It's nearly dark and Enid and Tobah have not come home yet."

"What? What do you mean? They were here for lunch, weren't they?" Her husband answered, "No, they never came back. I assumed you'd packed them a lunch."

Now Lucy was starting to panic. A Plinket had an extremely fast metabolism and must eat several times a day in order to survive. If Enid and Tobah had not been here for lunch then they were already in trouble if they had no food available to them out in the woods. "Oh no," she sighed, "go get Father Luther . . ." and then she started to feel faint.

Eric ran and found Cookie supervising the dinner crew and told him what he knew. "But they were here for lunch, surely?" Cookie said. "No, they weren't." said Eric. "I spoke to the other Gardeners and no one has seen Enid or Tobah all day long since this morning. They must be in trouble, Cookie."

Cookie thought for a minute and said, "By the time we could gather the rescue party it will be dark out. The whole rescue party would then be at the mercy of the forest animals. Go to the back entry and see if you can see them coming, we can't go out at night, you know this, Eric."

Eric turned and ran then, down the hall from the kitchen to the back entrance. He explained to the guard how his son and Tobah had not been back yet from the woods so the guard opened the door and both of them spilled outside and looked frantically from left to right, searching for the two Plinkets. Father Luther showed up just then and said, "What a shame it's getting dark."

Since neither one of them could be seen, though, Eric started to run full speed through the back yard. When he got to the edge of the woods he yelled into it, "Enid! Tobah! Where are you, it's getting dark!" There was not a sound but the chirping of the birds and the crickets, though. Eric was just about to walk further into the woods, a very dangerous thing for him to do, when a giant owl swooped down from a tree right toward him. He ducked just in time to miss the massive birds' beak and then ran full speed back to the house. He was a sitting duck in the dense woods, to any number of predators out here. He simply couldn't stay and risk it. He had to get word back to Cookie and hope he and Father Luther would allow a rescue party.

"If we'd had more daylight, yes, Eric, we wouldn't hesitate to send a rescue party," said Father Luther, "but now it's dark out and the night creatures are out." Eric knew this too well, but kept the owl incident out of the conversation. "He's my son Father!! I can't just leave him out there! And what of Tobah? He's our only Gatherer!"

Father Luther and Cookie looked at each other and Cookie shook his head, "It's too dangerous and you know it. You know the rules and why we have them set up in the first place. You're one of our Supervising Gardeners, Eric, we can't risk losing you to a predator no matter who it is in the woods."

Father Luther then took Eric's and Cookie's hands and said a prayer. "Heavenly Father, we pray for the safety of Enid and Tobah. Please see to their needs and bring them safely home. Amen."

Eric would get nowhere with the elder Plinkets and deep down he knew they were right anyway. Emotions were not to be brought into the equation when it came to whether or not to follow Plinket guidelines and rules. He didn't have any choice but to get his wife and tell her the decision she already knew they would've made. They could only hope that Tobah and Enid had the common sense to stay out of the outdoors, to find a cave or a tree with an opening at the bottom and hide until morning.

Father Luther was the clan's oldest Elder. He always had the last word on any decisions that affected the clan and he wasn't going to go against the rules for Tobah and Enid, just like he wouldn't break the rules for anyone left out after dark. It was too risky, too dangerous. And all the Plinkets knew the consequences of being out after dark – it was just not done!

Chapter Five

If anyone had told Tobah the trouble he and Enid would be in that Saturday, he wouldn't have believed them. He simply would never allow such a thing to happen and he would've told the Plinket who told him it that he was crazy. But it did happen and now he didn't know what to do except pray to God that everything would turn out okay. Enid was badly hurt but Tobah had stopped the bleeding. Laying there on the floor of the cave he looked like a little boy, Tobah was heartbroken and if anything happened to Enid he would never forgive himself.

He still can't believe it happened and he went over it again in his mind. They'd sat on the moss, eaten their snacks, were staring at the clouds, and then what? He woke up with a start to see Enid face to face with a shrew the size of a chipmunk. Enid had fallen asleep too but Tobah could tell he was definitely wide awake now! "Enid," Tobah said, "Don't move." And Enid sat perfectly still, staring at the yellow teeth of his new enemy. He could barely breathe as a matter of fact.

Tobah kept his eyes on the shrew while leaning over for his bow and quiver. He had the bow in one hand and an arrow in the other when the worst thing that could happen, happened and so fast. Just as Tobah pulled back the arrow the shrew pounced on Enid, who screamed in pain while being bitten on the shoulder. Tobah shot the arrow directly into the shrew's eye and killed him instantly. But the damage was done. Enid collapsed and fainted into shock. There was blood pouring out everywhere, oh my God where was it all coming from?

Tobah realized the mouse had severed an artery in Enid's neck and so he leapt into action. He zipped open his fanny pack and immediately grabbed the first aid kit inside. He found the bottle he was looking for and pulled the cork stopper from it and dropped a drop of the liquid onto Enid's neck in one swift move. The blood around the bite started to foam pink and bubble to twice its original mass. Tobah thought at first that it wasn't going to work, he thought he was going to have to drag Enid's dead body out of the woods and deliver it to his poor parents who would just die from grief at losing their only son.

But it did work, and the bleeding finally stopped. Tobah cleaned the wound, placed gauze over it and held it in place for a moment. Then he took off his own shirt and started to rip it into strips he could use to hold Enid's bandage in place. After that he had to make a plan. He thought about it for a minute but there was really only one thing to do. He pulled on his hair and jumped up and down in frustration. They were too deep into the woods to make it back before dark and if this shrew was already looking for dinner before dusk, there would for sure be many more to contend with after dark. They had no chance at all out in the open like they were.

Tobah picked up his bow and quiver and Enid's over his shoulder. Plinkets instinctually never left anything behind. If a human had found a tiny bow and quiver imagine how they would search and search until they found the owner! He picked Enid up under the arms and started to drag him to the cave. It was their only hope of surviving the night.

Tobah placed Enid's motionless body on some moss inside the cave, checked his breathing and his pulse, then went to look for water. Enid moaned then, and Tobah realized his back ached so much that he thought maybe he broke it. But of course that was impossible because then he wouldn't be able to walk, which he did over to Enid then. "Enid," Tobah said, "Can you hear me?" Enid moaned again and only partially opened his eyes. "You just rest, Buddy. You've been hurt but I got the bleeding stopped and you're going to be okay. Right now I have to try and hide us from night creatures so I need you to lie still and stay quiet, ok?" Enid moaned a third time but seemed to understand what Tobah had said.

Then Tobah got up and gathered up all the branches and twigs he could find and made a sort of lean-to inside the cave, next to the opening. He then took one of the slices of pumpkin bread out of Enid's fanny pack and ate half of it. He then lifted Enid's head up onto his lap, he was barely conscious, and fed him the rest of it. An act that kept them both alive through the night.

At dawn Tobah awoke to a start realizing he wasn't in his warm comfy bed but lying on the hard ground with Enid right next to him. "*Oh it wasn't a dream,*" he thought. He looked out toward the entrance of the cave and saw that the sun was coming up. There would be a rescue party coming, he knew, so he had to get Enid out of the cave so they could be seen. He took the last piece of pumpkin bread and, as he did the night before, ate half and gave Enid the other half. Enid swallowed the bread with difficulty and said, "Water. . ." Tobah said, "They'll be here for us soon, Buddy. They'll bring water and food." Then he gathered up all their belongings and pulled him up under his arms and started to drag him toward the entrance.

No sooner had he gotten Enid out that he heard the voices of Cookie and Eric. "We're over here," yelled Tobah. And then he collapsed to his knees, starving, thirsty, and remembered no more.

Chapter Six

Tobah woke up 2 days later in the infirmary wearing a hospital gown and having an IV in his arm. Sandy, the nurse, was there then and said, "Just rest Tobah, you're going to be fine." She came over and told Tobah what a brave thing he'd done by saving Enid's life. "Yeah, real brave, Doc. Leading my best friend out into the woods to be devoured by wild animals. I feel like a real hero," he said sarcastically.

Sandy said, "Enid told us what he remembers and how you killed the giant shrew that attacked you." Tobah looked up at him, "You mean who attacked Enid." Tobah said. And Sandy said, "And you. How do you think your ankle was bitten almost off?" She pulled the sheet back on the bed and Tobah was shocked to see the lower half of his left leg in bandages. What the. . . "I was bitten too?" Tobah asked disbelieving. "I don't remember that."

"Selective amnesia, Tobah. The shrew attacked you first, Enid hit it with an arrow but didn't kill it and it turned on him. Bit right through his shoulder. That's when you got the second arrow into him that did him in. Excellent shooting, by the way, straight into its brain. Killed him instantly. You have a future as a Hunter if you want it."

"No, no more hunting for me, in fact I may never leave the house again!" "Oh sure you will, Tobah," Sandy responded. "You love it too much not to go back. You saved Enid's life for sure though, you should feel proud of yourself for saving your friend. If you hadn't had the presence of mind to remember the pumpkin bread in Enid's fanny pack, the two of you would've died in the night."

Tobah shuddered at the thought and then found that he was so exhausted he couldn't keep his eyes open one minute more. He slept on and off in a drugged stupor for two more hours. Plinkets healed really fast, though and it wouldn't be long before Tobah was out gathering again.

He rested when he was told to, let Sandy change his bandages every day and did what he was told. In only two days he went from nearly having his foot bitten off to fully healed and recovered. The special liquid in the bottle Tobah had in the woods was what Sandy used to heal Tobah's foot and ankle. It was a magic elixir from ancient times that they made out of a special plant only the Plinkets could grow. It was grown in the green house and was the most important plant for them.

With Tobah just off of crutches he couldn't wait to get back out gathering. After he scarfed down his breakfast in lightning speed, he got up to leave and Cookie said, "Just a minute, Tobah. We need to talk before you leave the area." So he was stuck there until everyone was done eating. He was not happy about it, either.

After everyone had left the table there remained Cookie, Father Luther, and Tobah. Father Luther, the clan's oldest Elder, started the conversation; "Tobah, in light of past events I'm sure you will agree that you are in need of an apprentice now. We've been without a Gatherer for several days while your ankle healed and we're nearly out of many things. It's too dangerous for the clan to have to rely only on you when you could become incapacitated and not able to gather. I'm sure you agree with this, do you not?"

"Yes, sir, I suppose you're right." Tobah did not want an apprentice! He liked his freedom too much and his leisure time out in the house exploring and finding new things the clan can use. An apprentice would go blabbing to everyone how Tobah likes to lay on the landing in the sun, how dangerous that could be and what a slow and lazy Gatherer Tobah really is. They'll find out all his secrets!!

"Tobah," said Father Luther, "after your father died we allowed you to take over as Gatherer at your very young age because you'd been going after things with your dad for a while before," here he paused and bowed his head before continuing, "well, before the accident. You are really too young *today* to be gathering on your own, actually, but because your father was so good at his job and taught you so well, we allowed you to take over in his place. Do you remember how hard that was for you to do? You always knew you would be our next Gatherer but you thought you had years more to train with him."

Father Luther and Cookie both could see the disappointment on Tobah's face. "We have a proposal for you, Tobah," Cookie said. "We want you to train someone in your techniques until he's well enough trained to do the job on his own, and then you can go back to gathering on your own. You will just hold a one day training refresher course with your apprentice once per month. Now how does that sound?"

"Oh that sounds like a much better plan for me," Tobah said. "Thank you very much. And I want you to know that I do appreciate the privileges I've been given and the extra portions of food that go with the job and a larger cubby to live in and everything else, I appreciate it so much. But I do like my privacy when I'm out in the house and I don't believe anyone else would respect the humans as much as I do. That's one of the things my dad taught me that was so important. You have to be respectful of the people you're gathering from, and grateful for the things you take."

"Yes, Tobah, we understand. That's why we're allowing you to choose your apprentice yourself. Of course you would want to choose your friend Enid, however, because of the injuries he's sustained we don't feel he will ever regain the strength in his arm to be a Gatherer."

"Well," Tobah said, "If that's what Doc says then it must be true. Hmmm, I think then I will pick Karl. He's going to be almost as big as I am and he's already quite strong. I know his father wants him to be a Guard like he is, though."

Father Luther said, "We'll talk to his father and make sure he understands the importance of the decision to the clan. I'm sure he'll be honored to have his son as Gatherer under your tutelage. Afterall, he won't be gathering all the time – he will still be a guard, he will only be our Gatherer if something were to happen to *you*."

"You run along then and get to gathering for today, Tobah," Cookie said. "We'll take care of everything else."

"Okay, Cookie. And thanks." and off he went into the human house.

It was a grey and rainy day and as soon as Tobah saw the weather through the window, he didn't feel like gathering anymore. He felt like crawling under his covers and sleeping the day away. He could hear the wind outside the house, and what little bit of the treetops he could see from the kitchen floor were bent over to the point it looked like they would break off. But there were many things the clan needed today and he had a lot to do. Maybe next Off Day he would sleep in and be lazy.

Tobah had a very long list of things to get today and he was barely going to get done before the boys got home from school. He decided he'd get some of the heavy stuff first so he headed toward the pantry. He took off his rope and tossed it into the air over the door knob where it hooked right on. The end of his rope had a 3-prong hook on it that would catch on the rope thereby making a loop so Tobah could climb up. Then he put on his rubbery gloves, and started climbing. He could easily fit under the edge of the door by rolling under it but he needed the door open for the light so he could see what he was doing.

When he'd climbed up to the door knob he sat down on the shaft with one leg hanging over either side. Then, with his rubber gloves still on for grip, he spread his arms as far and wide as they would go, gripped the knob as tightly as he could, and heaved himself to the right. Now upside down, with his left foot barely reaching the door frame, he pushed on it with all his might with his rubber boot and it was just enough to get the door to unlatch. Then he heaved himself as hard as he could to the left and righted himself.

Tobah then climbed down the rope, pulled on the door and opened it until there was enough light inside for him to work. As dark as it was outside though, he had to open it really far. Then he took the rope in his hands and heaved it with a heavy swing to unhook the 3-prong hook and get the rope back.

Now he had to make his way up the pantry shelves. Tobah had a secret way he did this. His father had set up a special place for the hook to grab onto that the humans didn't even know was there. When his father was young and was a Gatherer with *his* father, he said that they should go into the pantry where there was so much more food than just the refrigerator. Tobah's grandfather told him what a silly idea it was, they could probably get the door open but even if they did, how would they climb up the shelves to gather?

That's where Tobah's grandfather had a brilliant idea to help his son's dream come true. And that's where they found out what kind of treasures the garage held. Grandfather went out to the garage alone one day without Tobah's father and came back with several small screws, a jeweler's screwdriver that he had to *drag* all the way back home, and about a foot of wire that he also drug behind him.

The next time they went out together, the two of them took a hand drill and one of the guards to help them. All guards are extra strong because they're the first line of defense against anyone or anything that might want to come through a door into the clan's home. Grandfather knew they'd need the extra strength of the guard to help them screw the screws in because Tobah's father was still young.

First, Grandfather threw the rope up and around a jar of spaghetti sauce on the bottom shelf so they could all climb up. Then grandfather drilled the holes for the screws *inside* the door frame, inside the pantry, where the humans would never see. Then Grandfather and the guard screwed the screws into the holes and wrapped wire securely around the two screws, leaving a loop of wire exposed for the hook to grab onto.

Because Plinkets are so light weight, even the heavy ones, the screws are still securely screwed into the door jams today and the wire is just as sturdy as it ever was. With practice (okay, LOTS of practice) Tobah hooks his hook over the wire every time on the first try. And that's what he'd just done to get to the bottom shelf.

Tobah knew he was lucky because his clan's human family was very neat and particular about things. The mom, Claire, put the groceries away very neatly and always in the same place, so Tobah knew where everything was in there. Tobah could, if he had to, find something in the dark in their pantry. He was grateful it was so neat and tidy.

The first thing he did was pull out his peanut butter spade and plastic bags and unscrew the lid of the peanut butter jar. Then he filled up his plastic bags with the stuff, tied them off, and shoved them into his backpack. Three very large plastic bags full of peanut butter. He knew Cookie would only expect two but Tobah knew they were low on things and there was a lot of canning to do to make up for what they'd had to use from the pantry while Tobah's ankle was healing. Three bags would make enough jars to last them a long time since not everyone ate peanut butter, mostly just the younger Plinkets.

Then Tobah took his rope and climbed up to the next shelf where he placed a packet of hot chocolate into his back pack. That would last the clan a long, long time. Next time he came out he would get another one, too, so they had enough stored up for the whole winter. Everyone liked hot chocolate!

Then Tobah climbed up one more shelf and put 2 butter crackers into his back pack. They were like the town house kind of crackers so they stuck out of his back pack a bit, but that was okay. The hot chocolate envelope kept them from coming out or breaking.

With his back pack on his back, Tobah climbed down to the bottom shelf where he rolled a can of tomato sauce over the edge of the shelf and BAM! onto the floor. He would roll this all the way home and that would be the end of his first trip out into the house.

Chapter Seven

When Tobah got back to the kitchen, he started to pull the things out of his back pack onto the counter like he always did. Cookie saw him and pulled out a chair and made him sit down immediately. He drew in his breath sharply, "Tobah, you're as pale as a sheet! Sit down, sit down." Tobah actually hadn't realized until he sat down how tired he was or how much his ankle and his back hurt.

Cookie took ice packs out from the freezer and put them on Tobah's ankle which he raised and placed on another chair in front of him.

"I'm fine, Cookie, just a little tired," Tobah said. But Cookie knew better - Tobah was one of those Plinkets who never complained about pain or illness. Cookie remembered one time when Tobah didn't make it to the dining room for lunch so he sent Sandy over to check on him. Tobah had a 120 degree fever and was sweating bullets but never told anyone he was catching ill. He wound up in the infirmary for a day and a half taking on fluids and being cooled down.

"Well," Cookie said, "you just sit here for a bit while I make you a sandwich."

Tobah said, "Thanks Cookie, but not peanut butter, ok? I kind of had some already." Cookie looked back, grinning at the bags of peanut butter on the counter.

In five minutes Cookie was back with a snack for Tobah, a cricket salad sandwich, potato chips, sweet pickles, and a chocolate cupcake – Tobah's favorite treat. Tobah exclaimed, "Cookie! How will I eat lunch after eating all of this?"

Cookie said, "You just eat it now and you can have smaller portions at lunch if you're still full. Or I can make you another large snack and you can skip lunch. Whatever you prefer."

"Alright," said Tobah, and he dove in and devoured his entire snack. He loved Cookie for taking care of him so good. After an extremely loud burp, Tobah said to Cookie, "Cookie, I feel much better, thank you. I'm fine. I have to get back out now."

He handed the ice packs to Cookie and left the kitchen, but not before he heard Cookie say, "Be careful Choo Choo. Come back if the pain gets any greater."

This trip Tobah went for the refrigerator. He gathered more butter, 2 wrapped slices of cheese, and 2 bags full of hot fudge sauce whose lid he almost couldn't get off today. He also filled up 2 bags with vanilla yogurt and rolled up another slice of bacon into his backpack.

As he whipped the rope up to get the hook off the metal shelf, the hook came flying at a weird angle and almost hit Tobah in the head! "Jeez, I guess I'm really tired today," he said. "I'll talk to Cookie, he'll tell me to go to bed for sure."

As Tobah struggled toward the door with his heavy backpack, he felt like he might faint. His hands were shaking and his knees were weak. Timothy opened the door for him and said, "Tobah, you are quite a sight. You should go see Sandy right away." "Gotta drop off the goods to Cookie first," said Tobah with a tired grin.

Cookie took one look at him and said, "Tobah, you go get into bed this instant! I'm going to have Sandy check on you, too, so expect her at your door." Tobah took off his backpack and left it on the kitchen counter for Cookie to unload, something he never did before, but he felt if he didn't lie down right away he really would faint. He slowly trotted off, limping, to his room, where he collapsed on his bed.

A few minutes later Sandy showed up at Tobah's room and gave him a thorough examination. His ankle was not healing as it should be and Sandy told Father Luther that Tobah would have to stay in bed for a couple of days. Tobah was exhausted from the efforts of gathering and must take two days off to rest and recuperate. That was actually fine with Tobah since he wasn't too keen on starting this apprentice training with Karl anyway.

That night Cookie had an apprentice from the kitchen bring Tobah his supper and after he finished it he fell into a deep sleep.

He was having the dream again:

There he was in the outdoors, all by himself. He had a bow and quiver on him so he must be hunting, even though he wasn't a Hunter. He felt the rush of excitement as he heard the heavy foot-steps coming toward him and when he looked up he saw a Tyrannosaurus!! It was like a million story building coming toward him. He screamed and ran. Not knowing what else to do, he decided he would try to acclimate – to blend into his surroundings and become kind of invisible. Like a chameleon. He knew it worked because of what the other Hunters had told him but Tobah never tried the magic before. He concentrated with all his might, closed his eyes so he wouldn't see teeth as the last thing he'd ever see, and did it. He blended in with the foliage so well that the dinosaur just walked right past him. "Well what do you know," he exclaimed. "It works!"

He looked around him then. There off in the distance was a smoldering volcano. The trees were taller than any trees he had ever seen. He saw other dinosaurs roaming in a field not so far away. He could smell the dead plant swampy smell of the ground. He heard pteranodons screeching in the air as they flew over him. It was so surreal and scary! He ended up walking a long, long way to get home to a tree where his extended clan family lived. His wife was disappointed that he didn't have any meat with him from the hunt, but thankful he was okay after his run-in with the tyrannosaurus. He was giving her a long hug when he woke up from the dream.

Confused and a little fuzzy headed, he laid there for a moment thinking about the dream. He had it very frequently, along with some other dreams he didn't understand. One of them had to do with a very large space rocket flying through space, holding hundreds and hundreds of Plinkets on it. He knew it was going home but he didn't know where that was. It was all much clearer when he was having the dream, not so easy to remember after he woke up. He decided he would talk to someone about it.

"That dream," said Father Luther, "is the story of our past. That's what all our dreams are, Tobah, so we don't forget where we come from." Tobah was shocked to hear this. He thought it was just a nightmare about dinosaurs. But Father Luther said, "We will gather the children on Sunday and I will discuss it with you all. It's about time we had the talk with the little ones and you are still a little one, Tobah!" Tobah blushed at this, he certainly was not a little one! But he couldn't show anger to Father Luther for calling him one.

Father Luther was in charge of the clans' moral health and wellbeing. He is called Father because he is a Priest and conducts their Sunday church services every week. He also teaches Sunday school after church and the whole clan participates. They all are of the same faith, there aren't different churches like for humans, they only have the one. We all have the same God though. When humans first started worshiping God the Plinkets were so pleased because it was one thing they had in common.

At breakfast that morning Tobah ate like he hadn't eaten in a week. Cookie said, "Well, your appetite is back to normal that's for sure. How's the ankle today?" Tobah said it was feeling much better and that he knew he could resume his full duties. "I'll be taking Karl with me out Gathering on Monday, Cookie," he whispered. "Wish me luck and patience." Cookie winked at him then and said, "You'll do just fine."

Father Luther tapped his glass at the breakfast table for everyone's attention. He cleared his throat and exclaimed, "Day after tomorrow, on Sunday, all the little ones will stay behind in the Sanctuary after church and we will tell the story of the Plinkets and where we come from. It's been a while since we had the talk and it's long overdue. Some of you have been having disturbing dreams and the talk will explain why." Everyone was talking in hushed whispers then, Tobah could hear them say, "What does it mean?" and "What is he talking about? What talk?" Father Luther said, "You will all understand after church on Sunday."

Everyone finished their breakfast and went off to work. Cookie's apprentices cleared the table and made the several trips it takes to get all the dishes to the kitchen. Then they loaded the dishwashers and

went back out for all the napkins and inspected the tablecloths to see if they needed to be replaced. They almost never did – Plinkets are very neat, as I've said, and messes or spills don't happen very often. Cookie changes them for the simple reason that he gets tired of seeing the same one all the time.

The apprentices started preparing lunch. The kitchen was always a very busy place, something always had to be done. They were having shrew stew, the same little rodent that bit Enid and Tobah. Eric went back for it and hauled it to the house after he and Cookie had gotten the boys back safe and sound. The meat department was sure busy that day boy. It was a huge shrew and it took hours to skin it and prepare the meat for storage. Cookie always had plenty of meat in the freezer and made into jerky in case they run out during the winter. The jerky would sustain them until spring when the hunters could go out and hunt again. They can't go out in the winter because of all the snow. Not only would they be buried past their heads by the snow, but they would leave tracks behind. Tracks that could be seen by humans.

This is the reason they keep the potted trees in the clan area in the green house instead of in the garden. Fresh citrus fruit, juice and jellies to eat all winter. The Plinkets had managed to hybridize their seeds so their plants produced fruit all year long. They were kept in a special room that was specially lighted all the time so the trees would think they were still outdoors. The bulbs are called full spectrum lighting and mimic the rays of the sun so fruit and vegetables will grow indoors. They also keep some potted vegetables that allow them to have fresh salads almost all winter. Tomatoes, cucumbers, squash, lettuces, all of those grow in big pots maintained by the Gardeners throughout the winter.

During the summer the harvests are mostly canned and put up so the clan always has food available in case of a catastrophe like a tornado or something taking out the garden. The potted vegetables also produce all year long so that they wouldn't starve until they could get the gardens replanted. It's really an ingenious system.

Cookie was busy in the kitchen making a list of things he needed in the next couple of days from Tobah when there he came, running into the kitchen out of breath. Tobah was frantic. "Cookie, I think I was seen!!! What am I going to do???" This wasn't one of Tobah's usual flubs, just a little mistake that could be overlooked or forgiven by others. This was so serious that it could jeopardize the clan itself. Cookie was gravely serious, the look on his face scaring Tobah even more than he already was.

"Tobah," Cookie whispered, "are you sure? Did you see him see you?" Tobah knew what he meant: were they shocked and surprised from their reaction to *him*? Or was it mere surprise at just being surprised?

Tobah couldn't be absolutely certain now. He had made a noise and saw the boy turn and look surprised, he started, jumped, and immediately looked toward where Tobah was standing. But Cookie was asking did he see you or was he just startled by the sound you made? Tobah was absolutely certain of one thing: as he took off and scrambled down the banister he knew the boy was still in his room. He knew he did not see him escape. And with his lightning speed, he was pretty sure he hadn't seen him. Pretty sure.

He looked at Cookie and with his bravest voice said, "I think I surprised him with the sound. I don't think he saw me. I acclimated right away when I made the noise." Cookie searched into Tobah's eyes and saw that Tobah was telling him what he truly believed. And then he rolled his eyes and started breathing again. "Tobah," he said, "this is very serious. You could have made it so that our safety was in jeopardy. Human boys are very curious and they don't stop looking for something that easily – I'm not telling you something you don't already know. Now, why don't you go lie down for a minute and catch your breath. I will tell Timothy to keep a fresh eye out for anything out of the ordinary but I imagine we're fine." And with that, Tobah left the kitchen feeling a little better. "The boy must be out sick from school," Cookie said.

The next day was an Off Day so he spent the day reading in his cubby. They had many books to read in the library and Tobah was always checking out new ones he hadn't read yet. He loved to read. He decided to go see Enid then and closed his book and put it back on its shelf.

Enid told Tobah, "Yes, I'm sure I'm ready to go back outside after what happened to us. We will just be more careful this time." So they parted ways to get their gear on. Tobah had special hiking boots that had a deep tread for walking around outside. And his utility belt held more stuff than Enid's did. Enid's only held a knife, cat repellant, a flashlight, and had a built-in fanny pack for storing food for the days trip or for bringing things back to the house.

They met up in the hallway outside the kitchen and saw Cookie inside. "Cookie, what can we bring with us to munch on today?" said Tobah. And Cookie took out a tray of sandwiches from the refrigerator for them to each grab one. They did and also a big red apple for each of them and they headed out.

Tobah thought he would feel trepidation about going back outside after such a traumatic event, but he felt fine. And Enid was in a fine mood. They hiked along next to each other, basking in the sunshine and noticing all the smells and sounds around them. The swampy smell of the ground, the smell of the flowers in the woods, the trees, it was all wonderful. Just then, a twig snapped. Tobah started and twisted around to see what it was. It was a large juicy squirrel. "Enid! Quick!! Get your slingshot ready!" and they both drew them back with rocks in them and pummeled the squirrel right between the eyes. Bang. Dead squirrel. "Good job Enid!" said Tobah. And they both grabbed part of its tail and drug it home for the meat department.

After they skinned the animal they cut big sections of meat up for the freezer and Cookie wanted to make some squirrel jerky today out of the rest of it. This was always a fun time for the apprentices because they got to eat pretty much as much of the meat as they wanted while they were working. The meat was taken, in sections, to the freezer for partial freezing. This made it much easier to slice for the jerky. Then after it was sliced it was laid out on big paper towels to dry. The little pieces of meat leaving a bloody circle on the paper, dried fairly quickly while Cookie prepared the jerky solution. 5 cups of soy sauce, 5 cups of Worcestershire sauce, garlic, onions, cayenne pepper and a few other ingredients went into a large bowl and the scraps of meat were then dumped into the solution and sat in it overnight. There always had to be room in the refrigerator for the big bowl to sit in it so the meat wouldn't spoil.

The next day Cookie took out the meat and laid it across oven racks for drying. The apprentices were always really happy to help with this part because they got to sample the meat after it had been marinated. It was soooo good! After the racks were laid up with all the meat, they were placed in the oven on a very low temperature with a fork stuck in the door for the air to escape. The meat dried in about five hours. It was a very long time-consuming job but the end result was the finest squirrel jerky in the world. Cookie tried gopher jerky once but it wasn't as good. Squirrel had no gamey taste like gopher does. Gopher roast has to be marinated for hours and hours to get that gamey taste out of it.

Chapter Eight

Sunday morning had finally come and Tobah didn't remember his dreams from the night before – and he was kind of glad. Dinosaurs were cool to look at in books but his dreams were so realistic they scared him to death. He was excited for after church to hurry up and be here so he could here "The Story" and be in the know like all the Elders and other clan members apparently were. All the little kids were excited too. So finishing his sermon, Father Luther said, "You are all invited to stay and listen to the story if you want to. I'm sure I'm not telling it any different from when you heard it as a child though." Many of the parents stayed behind to listen too. You could feel the excitement in the air!

He started, "The story I'm about to tell you is the whole history of our people from the dawn of time until now. It spans a time frame of 80 million years. So sit back and get comfortable and we are about to go on a little adventure."

He took off his church robe then and laid it across a pew so he was more comfortable and began to speak. "A long, long time ago, far, far away the Plinkets evolved into what we are today. We did not evolve into Plinkets on Earth however." There were gasps all around. "No, we evolved into Plinketts on the planet the humans call Mercury. We know it as Regis." He let this sink in for a moment and continued, "We evolved from apelike creatures into what we are now and there were no humans on Regis. There were all kinds of other animals – animals you have never seen or heard of because they are no more. Regis has moved too close to the sun and the atmosphere burned away. It was a beautiful planet once with oceans and islands and volcanos and all the same kind of land masses on Earth today. We loved our home very much. Today it is 330 degrees Fahrenheit - much too hot to live on and not even to visit."

"Our people were technologically advanced to a much higher degree than humans are now. We had spaceships that could cross space at light speed. We had airplanes and busses and trains and we had a thriving society. Then one day a scientist named James of the Colbert clan noticed a strange thing. Regis was getting close to the sun by approximately 100 miles per day. This didn't seem too much off course because it normally did move closer to the sun but not by that much every *day*. He deducted that we had to leave the planet in order to keep our species alive. We were going to have to find a new home in what the humans call the Milky Way Galaxy."

Father Luther continued, "Now some Plinkets didn't believe him. They wanted to stay behind and take their chances even though he warned it would be a hot horrible death as the sun started to get closer and closer and closer. They would not give in, though, and they were left behind."

"We built three special spaceships to carry us all to our new home and our scientists knew that home would be the planet Earth. Venus was much closer but much too hot to live there. Venus is more than 700 degrees Fahrenheit. Scalding hot! So we ended up leaving with only 2/3 of our population, leaving the foolish people behind who didn't believe the scientists."

"When we got to Earth the first thing we noticed is that it was much cooler than Regis. And it didn't take long for us to learn how to weave blankets from the plants that grew in the swamps. We also noticed the dinosaurs!" There were big gasps from the children now. The parents smiled. Father Luther continued, "Yes! Gigantic dinosaurs were on the planet we arrived at and no one knew it until we got here. They must have been evolving while we were busy perfecting light speed travel because we'd sent a pilot ship ahead to make sure the atmosphere really was right for us. They didn't report any dinosaurs, but nonetheless here they were."

"Of course running from them was an impossibility. Many Plinkets died from being eaten by dinosaurs and saber tooth tigers and pteranodons which are giant birds with teeth in their beaks. It was a very dangerous time for the Plinkets. We built our homes in the bases of tree trunks in the forests. The plant-eating dinosaurs only noticed the leafy vegetation on top of the trees, not the trunks, and the saber tooth cats were in for a surprise while we perfected our cat repellant. We lost many, many Plinkets to predators, though."

He stopped here as Cookie and some of the kitchen apprentices brought in sandwiches and fruit for everyone to snack on. No one realized how hungry they were they were all so engrossed in the story.

Then he continued, "We lived in our tree homes for many generations. First we learned how to mine ore metal without getting eaten by a dinosaur. Then we learned how to smelt ore inside a tree and not burn the tree down. Pretty soon we were in our Bronze Age and moving right along."

"Food was not really a problem for us. We of course brought all our seeds with us from Regis so we could grow our own fruit and vegetables. Which is a good thing we did! Look at the size of the human's orange tree or grapevine! We would never be able to harvest such things as these. So we made our gardens, the glass apprentices blew jars so we could can our harvests, the metal ore apprentices made metal lids for the jars, the Gardeners grew everything we needed to eat and there were plenty of large fat insects and small animals for meat."

"We were sorely lacking in things we had on our beloved Regis like electricity and modern appliances and such. And cars! It took a lot of walking to the ore mines and where the special papyrus plants grew that we used to make paper and blankets. Those plants don't grow here anymore in North America, the ice age wiped them out and they never did come back. But we used the skins from insects and small rodents to make all the clothing and boots we needed. It's not like we had to reinvent the wheel really. We already knew how to do all of these things from ancient times on Regis, it was only to find the resources."

"One day we noticed a very unusual thing. We saw a group of monkeys walking upright on both their hind legs! That's right. This was not seen back then so we were all surprised and amazed when they continued to do so. And over the years we came to see the dawn of man. *Enormous* creatures they were! But if we could live with dinosaurs around us we could live with humans too. We were careful not to be seen even way back then."

"Over the millennia we evolved too, became more adept at our weapon-making skills, learned how to survive an ice age, outlived many species of flora and fauna. We were really coming along. And then the humans started building structures instead of living in caves. We thought that was a great idea but instead of building our own we stayed in our tree trunks for a few more generations. Then we decided, as a people, not just as individual clans, that it was too dangerous for us to remain outdoors. There were more and more cats and wild animals that liked to eat us and we didn't have a repellant for all of them so we decided to move into the humans houses and just not tell them."

"So we planned and talked and planned some more and found that all of the structures the humans were building had a space in between the outside wall and the inside wall. And also between the sub-floor and the wood floor. It was perfect. We started to build our cubbies in these spaces and silently and slowly moved in with all of our stuff we'd learned how to create like dishwashers and washing machines and refrigerators. We tapped into their electricity and their water pipes so we had running water and could do everything the humans did."

"Through all of the trials and tribulations of planet Earth from the meteor that killed the dinosaurs and through the ice ages we sustained ourselves and survived. And now here we are today. We are still exploring space without the humans knowing because we believe one day the humans will destroy this planet. We will have to find a new home somewhere outside the galaxy and move there just like we did from Regis. We cannot move to Mars because there is no atmosphere and it's a dead planet. Jupiter, Saturn, Uranus and Neptune are all too cold. Plus, the only life we've found so far is some tiny sea creatures on one of Jupiter's moons. It'll be eons before there is intelligent life there."

"No, we need to find a planet with Earth's atmosphere, growing seasons, and gravitational specifics so we can live there as comfortably as we live here on Earth. Then we will take our giant spaceships to that planet and live there until who knows when. In the meantime, we have everything we need for life here. And we have a system of government and law within our clans, the Elders who keep passing things down from one generation to another so we don't forget, and we have God Almighty to help us through the rough patches."

"We have our own car manufacturing plants, we build our own dishwashers and refrigerators and microwaves, we have everything the humans have and then some. We have space travel! The humans have not yet found out how to travel at the speed of light so we are generations ahead of them in this technology. It will only be a matter of time before we find a suitable planet for us to move to."

After that Luther asked, "Does anyone have any questions?" Someone asked, "How come we don't have animals our size on Earth? We have our size plants and trees..." Luther said, "That's because when we moved here we only had enough room on the spaceships for Plinket food, not enough to feed all the animals too. Besides, we get by just fine eating crickets and mice and squirrels and all the other meat we have around us. We have the humans who supply us with fabric and paint and other useful tools we need. There is really no need for us to have brought our animals. Except for dogs. We do miss our dogs. We could not bring our pets with us when we left Regis and many of us were heartbroken beyond belief. It took many generations of Plinkets before we forgot what it was like to have a pet dog. Some of us have dreams about them and it brings great comfort and joy."

Tobah raised his hand. "Yes Tobah?" said Luther. "You said you would explain to us about our dreams." "Oh yes, of course. The dreams you have that are about Regis are actually hardwired into our brains so we never forget where we come from. Many Elders believe we are all reincarnated and actually lived a past life on Regis before being born on Earth and that it's ancient memories we are having. Dreaming about spaceships and dinosaurs is perfectly natural and welcome. It means you have not forgotten our long ago history and story."

"And with the son doing what the father did before him and the daughter doing what the mother did before her, we will never be without a Cookie or a Nurse or a Priest or any Elders. That's how we sustain ourselves and we can go on living here as long as the humans don't destroy the planet."

Bellah asked, "What do you mean by destroy the planet Father Luther? Will they blow it up?" He answered her, "No probably not although a nuclear holocaust is a real possibility. They have not evolved as highly as we have and still have wars with each other. They do not know how to be good will ambassadors for each other and to not kill and harm. But they will probably use up all of Earth's resources and kill her in that way. They are already poisoning the air and water and raping the land for coal and oil. They are foolishly digging in the ocean to find crude oil to run their cars and other machinery! Whereas we have electric cars, we do have to rely on humans for our electricity. We cannot have fields of windmills because they would be seen and we would be found out and we can't damn their rivers because they are too mighty."

Everyone sat there for a minute not saying anything, trying to let it all sink in. What a lot of information to receive all at once! Tobah, for one, was relieved to hear about how his dreams were normal. He was getting concerned about that.

"Any more questions children?" asked Father Luther. No one said anything else. It had actually gotten quite late into the afternoon and supper would be ready soon. Tobah loved the day he had today. What a great story. Father Luther said, "You will come up with more questions over the next few days. Just feel free to ask your parents or one of your Elders and they will explain it." Then he picked up his church robe and left the Sanctuary.

At the dinner table that evening everyone was talking a lot about the story. You could hear, "Oh, I get it!" and "That makes sense now!" and the atmosphere literally vibrated with excitement. Someone tapped their glass with their spoon and when everyone had quieted down, someone asked Father Luther, "Why can't we let the humans know we're here?" Suddenly everyone was asking, "Yeah, why not?" Father Luther cleared his throat and said, "Because they might try and keep us as pets. For those of you who don't know what a pet is, it's a small creature that lives in the house with the humans. It is a dog or a cat or a hamster or a guinea pig. These animals oftentimes live in a cage and are fed only when the human remembers to feed them. Would you like that?" There was dead silence around the table then. All the Plinket children looked at each other and started shaking their heads no and saying, "No we wouldn't like that at all." Father Luther was nodding his head in agreement, "No, none of us would like that."

After dinner Tobah went to his cubby and laid down on his bed to read more of the book he'd checked out from the library. He fell asleep while reading it and fell into a deep sleep, dreaming about dinosaurs and spaceships and table cloths and smiling in his sleep.